# Amanda Allan, Reporter

by
Tim Wall

Watermill Press

# Contents

# The Dating Service

"I'm worried about Stan," Nettie Rosenthal said to Amanda Allan. Stan Gordon was the editor of the *Smithtown News*. It was Thursday afternoon. The two reporters were in the office of the *News*.

"I saw him half an hour ago," Amanda

*"I'm worried about Stan,"* Nettie Rosenthal
said to Amanda Allan.

said. "He didn't seem to be sick."

"I'm not worried about his health," Nettie said. "He's as strong as a bull. He works twelve hours a day, seven days a week. As a matter of fact, that's his problem."

"It is?" asked Amanda. Even though she was a reporter with the *News*, she was only sixteen years old. Sometimes she was slow to understand the problems that older people had.

"Think about it," Nettie said. "He must be forty years old, but he's still not married. He's all alone, without a wife or a family."

"You're over thirty, and you're not married either," Amanda pointed out.

"It's not the same thing. I'm just waiting for the right man to come along. I still like to meet other people and go out on dates. Stan, though, is all wrapped up in his work. He won't even think about taking a night off."

"I think Mr. Gordon believes his job is more important than anything else," Amanda said.

"That's just what I mean," Nettie agreed. "Oh, the poor man."

Their talk was cut short by the voice of Stan Gordon himself. It came from down the hall and boomed through the building.

"*Amanda!* Where is that girl? Amanda, report to my office!"

Amanda hurried to Stan's office.

"I need you to cover a story right away," Stan said. "There's a new business that's opened in Smithtown. I want you to talk with the owner and write a story about it. You'll have to hurry, though. The place closes in an hour."

"I'll get right down there," Amanda

promised. "What kind of a business is it?"

Stan Gordon cleared his throat. "It's a dating service—one of those places that fixes up dates between single people."

"A dating service!" Amanda said. "Who would want to read a story about a dating service?"

"Plenty of people would," Stan said. "Besides, there's another reason for us to run this story."

"What reason?" Amanda wanted to know.

"Do I have to draw a picture for you? Newspapers make money from running ads. You remember that, don't you? If we run a story about this dating service, they will see how helpful it is to have their name in the paper. Then we can get them to put an ad in the *News* every week. Now do you understand?"

Amanda nodded. "I'll get right on the

story, Mr. Gordon," she said and quickly left the office.

A short while later, Amanda stood in front of the address Stan Gordon had given her. The shop had a new coat of paint. Over the window hung a sign that read, "Lonely Hearts Dating Service." Below it, another sign said, "Let Us Fix You Up."

The owner of the service, Stan Gordon had said, was Ms. Lola Anderson. Amanda found her inside the shop, sitting at a desk. Amanda gave Ms. Anderson her name and explained why she had come.

"I'll bet there are a lot of people who could use your service," Amanda said. She was thinking of what Nettie had said about Stan Gordon. "Your business should make a lot of money."

"Please, let's not talk about money,"

*Amanda stood in front of the address
Stan had given her.*

Ms. Anderson said. "I like to think of our service as a way of helping people. Just think of all the lonely people right here in Smithtown." Ms. Anderson lifted a stack of printed forms from her desk. "In only one week, all these people have come to us, seeking friendship, seeking someone who will understand them. We want to help these lonely people."

Amanda looked up from her notes. "How do you go about helping them?" she asked.

"Everyone who wishes to use our service fills in one of these forms," Ms. Anderson explained. She handed Amanda a blank form. "They answer questions about what they're like and what they're interested in. They give us their phone numbers. Then our computers match the people who would go well with each other."

Just then, the telephone rang. Ms. Anderson turned around in her seat to answer the phone.

Amanda should have been busy with her notes, but she couldn't help thinking of Stan Gordon. She looked at the blank form she held in her hand.

Ms. Anderson was taking a long time with her phone call. Amanda wrote Stan Gordon's name at the top of the form. She knew his telephone numbers at home and at the *News* office. She wrote these down. She filled in the blanks with some of the things she knew about Stan. Then she made up answers to the questions she wasn't sure about.

*After all,* she thought to herself, *I owe Mr. Gordon a favor. He might be mean at times, but he did give me the chance to be a reporter. Whenever I get into*

13

*trouble, he always backs me up. Why shouldn't I help him out?*

Amanda finished filling in the form. She slipped it into the stack on Ms. Anderson's desk.

Amanda went straight home after leaving the Lonely Hearts Dating Service. She wasn't due back at the *News* office until Monday. Over the weekend, she wrote up her story.

Monday, after school, Amanda hurried to the office. She had to type her story for the next edition.

Amanda slipped behind an empty desk. Nettie Rosenthal was sitting next to her. Right away, Amanda knew that something was wrong.

Nettie's face was pale. Her lips were stretched in a thin line. "It's really quite shocking," she said. "I've never known young ladies to act in such a fashion."

"Which young ladies?" asked Amanda.

"The ones who have been calling the office all morning, asking to speak to Stan. Two of them even came in person. They said they came to set up dates with Mr. Gordon. I never thought Stan was that kind of a man."

"Oh, it wasn't Mr. Gordon's idea," Amanda said. "It was my idea. I guess, in a way, it was your idea, too, Nettie." Amanda explained what she had done for Stan at the Lonely Hearts office.

Before Nettie could say anything, a voice ran through the halls. "Has Amanda come in yet? I want to see that girl right away!"

Amanda went to Stan's office. He was as angry as she had ever seen him.

"I don't know what's going on here," he said. "But I think I know who's at the bottom of it. This must have something

15

to do with your trip to that dating service, Amanda.

"I haven't had a moment's peace all weekend. I've had lonely hearts calling me every other hour. They're calling me here at the office, too. The girls who answer the phones are laughing at me."

The telephone on Stan Gordon's desk started ringing. He picked up the receiver.

"Hello. It's who? No, I don't want to talk with her about a date on Friday. I don't want to take any more calls all day. Is that clear, Ms. Henderson?"

Stan slammed the receiver into place. He stared at Amanda. "You've gone too far this time, Amanda Allan."

Amanda was saved by Nettie Rosenthal. Nettie had stepped into Stan's office.

"It's not Amanda's fault," said Nettie.

"I'm the one to blame. If I can speak to you for a moment, I can explain everything."

Stan looked from Amanda to Nettie, then back to Amanda. "You can go now," he said to Amanda.

Amanda returned to her desk. She couldn't understand what had gone wrong.

Finally, she began typing her story. She was still on the first page when Stan Gordon came by her desk.

"This story will be ready in an hour," Amanda told him.

"That will be fine," Stan said. "By the way, I'm sorry I sounded so angry just now. Let's forget that any of it happened, O.K.?"

Stan began to walk away, then returned to Amanda's desk.

"When you're finished with that story,

*"It's not Amanda's fault,"* said Nettie.
*"I'm the one to blame."*

just leave it on my desk. I won't be in my office this evening."

"Don't tell me you're going home early," Amanda said.

"No, I'm not going home." Stan cleared his throat. "As a matter of fact, I'm taking Ms. Rosenthal out to dinner."

# The King of Moravia

Stan Gordon called Amanda into his office.

"I have a big story for you," he told the sixteen-year-old reporter. "I wanted Nettie Rosenthal to cover it, but she called in sick. You're to go out to the home of Olivia Offenbach. Her cousin is coming to visit her today."

Amanda made a face. "That's a big story?" she asked.

Stan Gordon's face turned red. "Now don't start in again, Amanda. This story has to be handled in just the right way. Mrs. Offenbach's cousin is coming all the way from Europe. Her cousin, in case you've forgotten, is the King of Moravia."

"I do remember Mrs. Offenbach," Amanda said. "She's that rich old lady who's always boasting about what an important family she comes from."

"Mrs. Offenbach is a leading citizen of Smithtown," Stan Gordon said. "I don't think it's a good idea for you to call her a 'rich old lady.' Her cousin is also quite important. Moravia is a very small country, and it's no longer ruled by the royal family. But a king is a king."

"I guess it would be interesting to meet a king," Amanda said.

"Of course it would. Just remember, you have to be careful with Mrs. Offenbach. She's very excited about the king's visit. She's never met her cousin before. She called me up herself to make sure I was sending a reporter."

Stan Gordon hesitated. "Now, I know you like to do things your own way, Amanda. It's often worked out well. But this is different. I want you to be very polite to Mrs. Offenbach and to the king. I want you to write nice things about them."

"Yes, Mr. Gordon. I understand."

"That's better," Stan said. "I'm sending Luke with you to take pictures. He'll drive you in his car."

Mrs. Offenbach lived on an old estate, outside of town. Luke and Amanda

*Mrs. Offenbach lived on an old estate,*
*outside of town.*

drove past large houses, wide green lawns, and beautiful gardens. Then Luke turned down the drive which led to Mrs. Offenbach's house.

A servant answered the door. Mrs. Offenbach was behind him, looking over his shoulder.

"We're from the *News*," Luke said.

Mrs. Offenbach smiled. "I'm so glad you could come," she said. "Please come into the drawing room. Sutherland will bring you tea and some sandwiches. I'm expecting my cousin to arrive in a little while."

Luke and Amanda found a couch in the drawing room. Sutherland, the servant, brought out tea in a silver pot and a tray with sandwiches cut into tiny pieces. Mrs. Offenbach fluttered in and out of the room. She was becoming more excited with each minute that went by.

Finally the king arrived. A car that was black, shiny, and very long pulled up to the house. The driver, in a gold-trimmed uniform, stepped out. He marched around to the car's back door and opened it. A tall man in a uniform with medals and ribbons, and even more gold trim, came out.

The driver clicked his heels. "His Majesty, the King of Moravia!" he announced.

Mrs. Offenbach rushed forward and hugged the king. Luke snapped pictures.

The little group returned to the house. Mrs. Offenbach led them back to the drawing room.

"What a lovely house you have, my dear cousin," the king said. He looked around the room at the old paintings on the walls, the velvet curtains, and the gold and silver vases. "Its beauty, however, fades before that of our gracious

*A tall man in a uniform with medals and ribbons came out.*

and honored hostess."

Mrs. Offenbach blushed in delight.

"But where are my manners?" the king said. "Allow me to present my trusted driver and right-hand man, Rufus."

The driver of the car stepped forward and made a short bow.

Mrs. Offenbach was delighted again.

The king and Rufus left with Mrs. Offenbach to tour the rest of the house. Sutherland left to prepare the guest rooms.

Luke looked at his watch. "Stan wants me to take some pictures back in town," he said to Amanda. "I might as well drive over and take them right now. You can stay here and talk with His Majesty. I'll be back in an hour to pick you up." Luke took a tiny sandwich and went out the door.

When Mrs. Offenbach returned, the king and Rufus were no longer with her.

"His Majesty wanted to stretch his legs," she explained. "The poor dear has had such a long drive from his hotel. He's out with Rufus, looking over the grounds."

Amanda decided it was a good time to talk with the king. She went out to the yard behind the house.

Amanda walked past flower gardens, a lily pond, and several marble fountains without seeing anyone. Then she heard voices from behind a clump of tall bushes. They were the voices of the king and Rufus. Somehow, though, the tone of the voices had changed.

"Do you really think we have them fooled?" she heard Rufus say.

"Of course they're fooled," the king replied. "Mrs. Offenbach has never met her cousin before. She's so worked up right now, she'd believe the milkman was a king. That servant is about eighty years old and can hardly see anymore. The guy taking pictures couldn't care less about who we are. And that reporter – she's just a kid. She's the last one we have to worry about."

"I guess you're right, George," Rufus said. "Things are working out just fine. We have the real king tied up in his hotel room."

George, the "king," laughed. "All that's left now is the easy part. We keep up our act for the rest of the evening. Then, in the middle of the night, when the old lady is asleep, we clean out the house. Those paintings alone are worth thousands of dollars. We load everything into our rented car, and we're gone. We can rob everything we want without going to the trouble of breaking into the house."

"I've got to hand it to you, George," said Rufus. "You've sure got this one figured out."

Amanda had heard enough. Mrs. Offenbach had to be warned! The young reporter ran back to the house and found Mrs. Offenbach in the drawing room.

"Mrs. Offenbach, ma'am, there's been a terrible mistake," Amanda said. "That king is nothing more than a crook."

Mrs. Offenbach fixed a cold stare on Amanda. "Young lady, that is an insult to my family and to the Royal House of Moravia. I shall certainly report this to the editor of your newspaper."

"No, you don't understand," Amanda said. "That man out there is not your cousin!"

Mrs. Offenbach became even more angry. "Now you have the nerve to question my ties to the royal family." Her eyes looked upward. "To think that I should have to bear such insults in my own house."

Mrs. Offenbach was saved from further insults by a voice from the door of the room.

"I'm afraid the young lady is right," the voice said. Mrs. Offenbach and Amanda turned around. The two visitors stepped into the drawing room.

"You see, we have borrowed these uniforms from your cousin," the "king" said. "I don't know how this girl discovered our secret, but it doesn't make any difference. It just means that our plans to rob your house will have to be pushed ahead a few hours. Now, if you will please sit down on that couch, my trusted right-hand man will tie you up."

It was all too much of a shock for Mrs. Offenbach. She slid to the floor in a faint.

"You're not going to get away with this!" Amanda warned.

The "king" laughed in a nasty way. "Who's going to stop us? You?"

"I don't have to," Amanda said. "While you've been talking, someone's come in the door behind you. He has the drop on you right now."

George laughed again. "You don't fool us with that old trick. You want us to turn around so you can run out the door while we're not looking. Well, it won't work."

This time, however, the "king" was wrong. Old Sutherland had, in fact, come in the door. He heard what was being said, and he picked up one of the silver vases. He raised it in the air and brought it down on George's head. The thief fell to the floor under the force of the blow. Amanda rushed forward and kicked Rufus in the shins.

Rufus hopped around the floor in pain. The "king" lifted himself from the carpet. But Sutherland came after him again, waving the vase in the air.

"Let's get out of here, George!" Rufus yelled. The two men made a rush for the door. In seconds, Amanda and Sutherland heard the slam of the car door. The engine came to life, and the car sped away.

A few minutes later, Luke returned to the house. Amanda had just finished putting through a call to Stan Gordon. Sutherland was holding smelling salts under Mrs. Offenbach's nose.

"Did His Majesty go for a drive in the

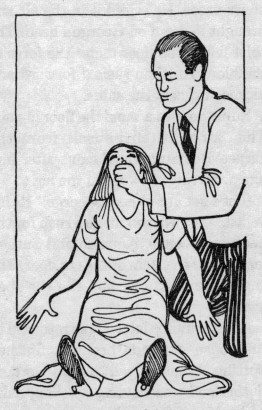

*Sutherland was holding smelling salts under Mrs. Offenbach's nose.*

country?" Luke asked. "He and Rufus drove past me as I was coming up the drive. They must have been going ninety miles an hour."

"I believe, sir," said Sutherland, "that His Majesty has gone for a very long drive in the country. If I don't miss my guess, he'll be going as far as the state line."

# Stranger at the Wedding

"You're giving me this story just because I'm a girl!"

"That's not true," Stan Gordon told Amanda. "You're getting this story because you're sixteen years old. You can go back to being a newsboy if you don't like it."

"If I did, I'd be a news*girl*, not a news-*boy*," Amanda huffed. "Why can't I cover the bank robbery? It just happened this morning. And they still haven't caught the thief. I've looked at all the reports that came in from the police."

"Don't be silly," said Gordon. "Harrison's covering that story. That's a front-page story, and Harrison's my best reporter. I need you for the Shelby wedding. The Shelbys are the richest family in Smithtown. Their daughter is marrying Dick Williams. His family owns the Williams Steel Company. In this town, that's big news."

Amanda sighed. "All right. I'll cover the stupid wedding. But only as a favor."

Stan Gordon smiled at the girl. "That's better. The wedding's at the church on Franklin Avenue. I've already told them you're coming."

*"Charlene!" said Amanda. "What are you doing here?"*

At the church, Amanda met Charlene, one of her friends from high school. "Charlene! What are you doing here?"

"Hi, Amanda," Charlene grinned. "I'm here with my parents. They're friends of the Shelbys, you know."

"My word," Amanda drawled. "I had no idea you moved in such circles."

"Oh, cut it out," Charlene said. "Come on, the wedding's about to start. We can sit together."

The wedding march began. Charlene looked up at the young bride as she passed. "Isn't she beautiful?" Charlene whispered.

"Her? She has crossed eyes," Amanda said. "And her ears stick out."

After the wedding, Amanda caught Charlene in the crowd. "Hey, you've got to help me," Amanda said. "I need the names of the important people here."

"Why don't you come to the reception with me?" Charlene offered. "We can get the names there. You can come in the car with my folks."

The Shelbys lived in the center of town. They had a large, brick house. The lawn was cool and green under tall trees. In the main room of the house, the floor was polished to a shine. A band played soft music.

Amanda was busy writing down the names of the guests. The mayor was there, a banker, a noted author. The list went on and on.

"Who's that man — the tall, dark one — over there?" Amanda asked her friend. "I've seen his face before."

Charlene frowned. "I don't think I've ever seen him."

Amanda went back to her list. Her eyes, however, kept returning to the

*"Who's that man?" Amanda asked her friend.*

face of the tall stranger. He stood by himself, not talking to anybody.

"No one I've talked to knows who he is," Charlene reported a few minutes later. "I asked everyone—my parents, the mayor, the manager of the bank . . ."

"The bank! That's it!" Amanda's eyes were wide. "Charlene, I've got to get to a phone."

Mrs. Shelby was shocked when Amanda explained what the phone call was for. She wasn't sure if she should believe the young reporter. Finally, Mrs. Shelby showed Amanda to the telephone.

The police arrived in plain clothes. They checked the face of the stranger with the pictures they had brought. He was taken away quietly. The wedding guests hardly noticed.

Back at the office of the *Smithtown News*, Amanda talked with Stan Gordon.

"All right, how did you know he was the bank robber?" asked Stan.

"When he held up the bank, his picture was taken on one of those hidden cameras. I saw it in the reports the police sent to the *News*."

"But what in the world was he doing at a wedding party?" Stan asked.

"I guess he wanted to lie low until things had quieted down—maybe until he could meet a friend with a car. And who would have thought of looking for a bank robber at a wedding reception?"

"Nobody," Stan said. "Nobody except a sharp newspaperman."

"Newspaper*woman*," Amanda corrected.

"Anyway, you should talk to Harrison so he can get the story."

"I'm way ahead of you, Chief. Here it is. I've already written it."

Gordon looked at the typed pages.
"Well . . . this might do," he said.

Gordon looked at the typed pages. "Well...this might do. You'll get your ten dollars in the morning."

"Not for a Page-One story, sir. A Page-One story is worth fifty."

Gordon dropped the papers onto his desk. "It seems to me," he said, "that there was more than one thief at that wedding."

# A Work of Art

"Amanda!"

"Yes, Mr. Gordon?"

"Don't 'Yes, Mr. Gordon' me! And don't waste that sweet smile on me, either. What on earth are you doing?"

Amanda and Fred Jenkins, the man in charge of printing, were standing by what looked like a small, metal tree.

"Mr. Jenkins is making a camera stand," Amanda explained. "It's for my brother. Mr. Jenkins just took some of the metal scraps that are lying around—"

"Mr. Jenkins is supposed to be putting this week's paper to press," Stan Gordon boomed. "You both might have forgotten, but this is a newspaper office. You remember, don't you, Jenkins?"

"I'll get right on it, Mr. Gordon." Jenkins smiled at Amanda and hurried away.

Stan Gordon turned toward Amanda. "And you," he said, "are supposed to be at that art show."

"But the show doesn't start for an hour."

"Once the show starts, Mr. Higginbottom will be talking with the writers from the big city papers." Stan Gordon strode toward his office. Then he stopped

47

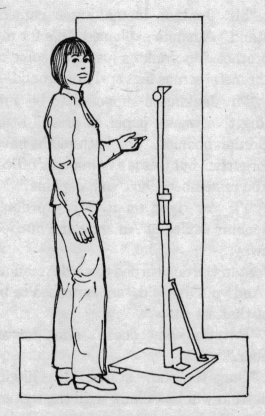

*"Mr. Jenkins is making a camera stand,"*
*Amanda explained.*

and turned to Amanda. "While you're going, you can take that safety hazard with you."

Amanda carried the camera stand with her to the art show. The sign in front of the gallery said, "Opening Today: The Works of Harrison Higginbottom."

Amanda knocked, but there was no answer. She pushed the door open and walked down the hall, which led to a large, dark room. Amanda put down the camera stand and called out, "Mr. Higginbottom!"

A moment later, the lights switched on. A middle-aged man in bib overalls came out from a back room. He wore wire-framed glasses. The top of his head was bald, but from the sides and the back, long hair fell to his shoulders.

"I'm from the *News*," Amanda said.

"Ah, yes," he said, "Miss Allan, the

49

reporter – and so young. I am Harrison Higginbottom. Allow me to take your coat." Harrison hooked Amanda's coat upon a wooden pole with iron spikes. A sign at its base read, "Anger."

The artist drew a red handkerchief from his pocket. He took off his glasses and wiped them. "This is the first show I've had on my own," he said. "I suppose I shouldn't tell you that."

Harrison was walking across the floor. Without his glasses on, he bumped into a huge beach ball. Amanda saw the beach ball's title, "Star Trip II."

Harrison put his glasses back on and continued, "It's quite important that this show turn out well. It could mean more work, more jobs. I could even move out of my mother's house."

"How will you know if it turns out well?" Amanda asked. She started to sit

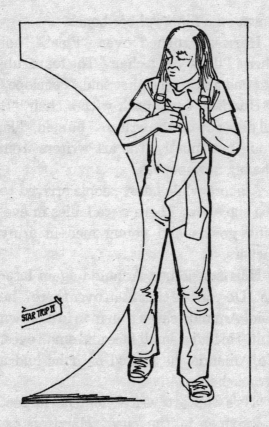

STAR TRIP II

*Without his glasses on, Harrison bumped into
a huge beach ball.*

down on a foam-rubber bench.

Harrison rushed over. "Please, not there. I'll get you a chair." The foam rubber had a sign on it that said, "Penelope."

Harrison came back with a chair. "It all depends on the writers," he said, "like you—but mostly, the art writers from the big newspapers."

A short while later, people arrived to see the show. There were ladies in evening gowns and young men in army jackets.

Harrison joined Amanda again later on. "Do you see that man over there?" he said. Amanda saw a thin man in a brown suit. He had a small face and small eyes. To Amanda, he looked as if he had a stomachache.

"He's the art writer for the largest newspaper in the city," Harrison explained. "When he writes something,

*People arrived to see the show.*

everyone else goes along with it."

The little man was walking around the room with a frown on his face. All of a sudden, he stopped. Amanda saw him start to smile. He took out a pad. His pencil wiggled back and forth across the page.

In the corner, where she had left it, was the camera stand. The little man looked at it as he wrote.

Harrison rushed toward the art critic. Amanda followed.

"I don't see a title to this piece," the writer said.

Harrison's mouth opened and closed, but no words came out.

"I believe Mr. Higginbottom told me it was called 'Safety Hazard,'" Amanda said.

The writer beamed. "Quite so, quite so. One almost trips over it. I'm starting to see the direction in your work, Harrison. It's fresh, pointed."

When Amanda returned to the *News* office, Jenkins had just finished the run of the printing press.

"Oh, Mr. Jenkins," Amanda said. "There's somebody who would like to meet you. He wants to know if you have the time for an extra job."

# The Missing Steam Shovel

Stan Gordon looked at the telephone receiver he was holding. He put it back in its cradle.

"Amanda," he said, "I just got a tip on a story. Could you walk over to the police station and cover it?"

"Sure," said Amanda. "What's it about?"

Stan Gordon seemed at a loss for words. "It seems the Ajax Building Company is missing a steam shovel. They think someone stole it."

"Why would anyone want to steal a steam shovel?" Amanda asked.

"I don't know, Amanda," Stan said. "If I knew these things on my own, we wouldn't need reporters, would we? Now, get on this story."

"Yes, sir," Amanda replied.

Mr. Clyde, of the Ajax Building Company, was already at the police station when Amanda arrived. The police chief was talking to him. "Are you sure you didn't just lose track of where you left it?"

"It's a twelve-ton machine," Mr. Clyde said, "and it's fifty feet tall. You don't lose something like that."

"When did you first notice it was missing?" the chief asked.

Mr. Clyde was becoming angry. "Last night, it was left at the grounds we're building on. This morning, it was gone."

"Could you describe what the steam shovel looks like?" The police chief was taking notes.

"It's a steam shovel! Your men should be able to tell one when they see one." Mr. Clyde shook a finger at the chief. "I want action. What kind of police force do we have when you can't even leave a steam shovel out overnight? I don't mind telling you the city board will hear about this." Mr. Clyde slammed the door as he left.

"What are your orders, Chief?" one of the officers asked.

"Set up road blocks," the police chief

*"When did you first notice the steam shovel
was missing?" the police chief asked.*

commanded. "I want every road out of town covered. Don't let any steam shovels slip through. And have someone question the neighbors. Find out if they heard anything during the night."

"Heard anything like what?" an officer asked.

"Like someone driving away in a steam shovel, of course."

Amanda walked out of the station, thinking. It seemed to her there was only one place a fifty-foot steam shovel could be hidden—the old gravel pit outside of town. If she was right, she wanted to be the first to get the story.

A winding dirt road led to the gravel pit. As Amanda approached, she heard the sound of heavy machinery.

Amanda reached the rim of the pit and peeked over. The steam shovel was there. It was big and yellow and said

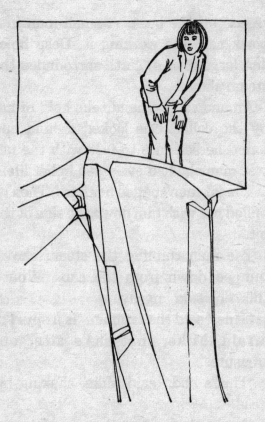

*Amanda reached the rim of the pit and peeked over.*

"Ajax" on the back. A small man in a black cap was working it. Deep holes and large piles of earth surrounded the steam shovel.

Amanda felt a hand take hold of her by the collar. She looked around and found herself face to face with the fattest man she had ever seen in her life.

The fat man tugged her hard. Then he pulled her with him down the side of the pit.

The man running the steam shovel jumped down from the cab. "What's this?" he said angrily.

"This," said the fat man, "is a spy. I'm afraid, Mike, that she's after our treasure."

"That's bad," said Mike, shaking his head.

"I am not after your treasure," Amanda said. "I don't know anything about any treasure. And take your hands off me."

"My dear girl," the fat man said, "surely you don't expect us to believe that you know nothing of the Farberman treasure?"

"The *who* treasure?" Amanda said.

"I think she's on the level," Mike said. "I don't think she knows anything."

"Farberman," said the fat man. "Fifty years ago, he was a very rich man in this town. He owned these gravel mines, among other things. But he was a strange old man. When he died, he didn't leave a penny to his family — not a penny. In fact, no one knew what became of the huge Farberman fortune."

The fat man threw his chest out proudly. "I, however, looked into some of the late Mr. Farberman's papers. They led me to believe the old man buried his fortune right here, in this gravel pit."

"That doesn't give you the right to the treasure," Amanda pointed out, "or to steal a steam shovel, for that matter."

"Please." The fat man held up a pink hand. "Not steal — borrow. We only wish to make use of the machine for one afternoon.

"We tried picks and shovels first, of course." The fat man sighed. "But Mike is not the biggest of men. And I, to my sorrow, am not of a build that lends itself to such labor."

Then, brightness returned to his face. "As for the right to the treasure, it seems that right belongs to those who can get their hands on it."

"You'd better be ready to explain all this to the police chief," Amanda said. "The whole police force is looking for

*"We only wish to make use of the machine for
one afternoon,"* the fat man said.

you at this very moment."

Mike shook his head again and said, "That's bad."

"All the more reason for us to make haste," the fat man said. "I think it best, young lady, that you remain our guest for the afternoon."

Two hours later, a metal clang was heard above the roar of the steam shovel. An iron box showed through the earth.

"The Farberman fortune!" breathed the fat man.

Mike broke the box open. It held only a piece of paper.

The fat man shut his eyes and said to Mike, "Read it."

"'To Whom It May Concern,'" Mike read. "'If you're greedy enough to have found this, you deserve all the trouble you've gone through. That goes for my money-hungry family, too. If you want my fortune, you'll have to keep looking. Signed, A.G. Farberman.'"

The fat man groaned.

"Where do you think the dough really is?" asked Mike.

"Who knows?" said the fat man. "Maybe at Farberman's salt mine in Ecuador, or on his cattle ranch in Australia." He dusted off his hands. "There's no use crying over our ill luck. Shall we continue the search, my friend?"

The fat man turned to Amanda. "Forgive us for bidding such a hasty farewell. It would be difficult if the police paid a social call just now. Unless, of course, you wish to join us."

"That's all right," Amanda said. "I have my own things to do, such as reporting a missing steam shovel."

# A Love Too Brief

"Our love is over," Cheryl Landstrom said. "It burned for a few bright moments, then it was gone."

"Yuck," said Amanda, "you could put that in a poem."

"I did," Cheryl said. "I wrote it last week."

"Well, what makes you think you and Tom are breaking up anyway?" Amanda asked. "You two have been going together for the last three months. That's a long time."

"Oh, there are little things that only a woman would notice—the faraway look in his eyes when I talk with him, the softness that's gone from his touch."

"Gee," Amanda said in wonder, "you notice all those things?"

"Of course I do. Besides, Tom hasn't taken me out for three weeks now."

Amanda and Cheryl were walking together through the high school. Their path took them across the main hall of the school.

"Tom's just getting out of English," Cheryl said. "When he comes this way to get to his geography class, you'll see what I mean." Cheryl was right. A few seconds later, the two girls saw Tom heading in their direction.

He was with three other guys. They were talking about the last basketball game of Smithtown High's team. Tom was hooking one of his arms over his head to show how the game-winning shot had been made. They were all talking in loud voices and laughing.

As Tom passed by, he glanced at Amanda and Cheryl. "Hi, Amanda, hi, Cheryl. Talk to you later," he said, then he went back to acting out the basketball game.

"I think I see what you mean," Amanda said.

Neither girl spoke as they continued down the hall. Then, Amanda broke the silence. "I'm sorry about you and Tom," she said. "But I was thinking about the poem you wrote. The newspaper that I

*Amanda and Cheryl were walking together
through the high school.*

work for prints a poem each week. Anyone living in Smithtown can send one in. You seem to have a way with words. If your poem is any good, they'll print it. It's a thrill to see what you've written in print. It might cheer you up."

Amanda hardly saw Cheryl again until the next week. Cheryl and Tom were sitting together at a table in the school lunchroom. As Amanda hurried over, she saw Cheryl speaking to Tom. Tom was bent over, wolfing down his food, nodding from time to time.

Amanda sat down across the table from them. Along with her books, she held a copy of the *Smithtown News*. "Cheryl, look. They put your poem in the paper. See, here it is—'Days of Love Gone By.'"

Tom pushed his tray of food away. "Let me see that," he said. He placed the newspaper on the table in front of him.

"Oh, Cheryl, it's so exciting," Amanda said. "See, there's your name—'by Cheryl Landstrom.'"

"Say, what is this?" Tom said. He read from the newspaper, "'Our love is over. It burned for a few bright moments, then it was gone.'"

"It's good, isn't it?" Amanda said.

"That's from a part of my life that's in the past," Cheryl said as her face took on a look of silent suffering.

"In your past?" said Tom. "Who is this guy?"

Before she could speak, Amanda felt a kick from under the table.

"It broke his heart when we had to separate," Cheryl said. "His father had to move to another town because of his business. Of course, the poor boy still writes to me."

*"Say, what is this?" Tom said.*

Tom went back to the poem. His lips formed the words as he read to himself.

Cheryl stood up. "I've got to run, Amanda," she said. "It's just about time for my next class."

Tom jumped up from his chair. "I'll walk with you to your class," he said, grabbing Cheryl's books. "I have some free time." As they left, Amanda heard Tom telling Cheryl about the new movie that was showing downtown.

Amanda looked at the newspaper that was still lying open on the table. *That Cheryl Landstrom certainly has a way with words,* she said to herself.

# The Movie Star

"Just think," Marcie was saying. "He's right here in Smithtown. So close you could almost reach out and touch him. *Him!*"

It was a rainy Saturday afternoon. Marcie, Ellen and Amanda were spending the day talking and listening to their

*"Just think," Marcie was saying. "He's right
here in Smithtown."*

favorite records.

On the floor lay a copy of the *News*. The back page had a short report on Michael Adonis. He was in the Smithtown General Hospital, it said. It was no cause for alarm, just a checkup for some pains he had felt while on vacation.

Michael Adonis was one of the brightest stars to come up in the last few years. His last two movies had broken box-office records across the country. His name was in the show-business columns almost every day.

"You could interview him for your paper, Amanda," Ellen suggested.

"Not likely," said Amanda. "His room will be shut up tight. They wouldn't let the Queen of England in."

"That's never stopped you before," Ellen said.

"I think Amanda's scared," said Marcie.

"Scared? Me, scared of that stuck-up featherbrain? You'll have to do better than that!"

"I think so," said Marcie. "You could get in if you wanted to. You could act like a hospital volunteer, and then go up the back stairs.

"I think you're right," Ellen said to Marcie. "I think Amanda's scared."

In Smithtown General Hospital, Michael Adonis lay in bed, staring at the cracks in the ceiling.

It was funny. The pain didn't bother him so much anymore. Now he knew what that pain meant and what the doctors had meant when they had looked away whenever he had asked them questions.

He didn't mind being alone now, either. Before, he had been afraid to be alone. Now he welcomed it.

Michael heard someone come into his room. A young girl walked around to where he could see her. "I took my pills half an hour ago," said Michael.

"I'm — I'm not a nurse," the girl said. She tried to stand up taller. "I write for the newspaper — the *Smithtown News*."

"Then get out," he said. "Now. Not in five minutes, not in five seconds, now."

Then he saw that the reporter was about to cry. "Hey, honey. Don't take it like that. You can't go getting so upset over what an old snake like me says."

Amanda closed her mouth, which had fallen open. "Don't you call me 'honey,'" she blazed. "I'm not your honey."

Michael Adonis laughed. "The old fighting spirit, eh? That's better. You stick with that. You'll need it. All right, go ahead, ask me your questions. There's a chair over there."

*"I'm—I'm not a nurse," Amanda said.*

Amanda realized she hadn't thought of any questions. She sunk into the chair. "What's it like to be a movie star?" she tried.

Michael Adonis didn't laugh the way she was afraid he would. He turned over and went back to looking at the ceiling.

"Dreams," he said. "You spend half your life making dreams that other people are supposed to like. But in the end, nobody's happy. They're not the dreams real people have. That's all my life has been — one big dream. And this is one I'd like to wake up from."

"But you make a lot of money, don't you, Mr. Adonis?"

He turned on his side and looked at Amanda. "Yeah, I can't complain about the money. It does make a difference. At least, for me it did. My family used to have so little of it.

"Take my father. He worked in a factory. Most people don't know that. I guess it'll be your exclusive. He made real things, not dreams. Things people could really use. And he died broke. He owed money on the house. They took the car away before they buried him. . . . Say, aren't you taking notes? What kind of reporter forgets to take notes?"

They talked for half an hour more. Then Michael Adonis said the pills were making him sleepy.

"You write that up well," he said. "I'll be looking for your story in the—what did you say the name of your paper was? Here, write it down for me."

Amanda wrote the story up that night. And she knew, right away, her story was special. It wouldn't show his fans the Michael Adonis they were expecting to see.

*"I'll be looking for your story,"*
*Michael Adonis said.*

In next week's edition of the *Smithtown News*, the public would read about the real Michael Adonis—not the carefree superstar, but an angry young man who was terminally ill.

# A Rough Life

For weeks, it had been very cold. The snow that had fallen had become frosted and hard. Even when the sun was out, temperatures were well below freezing.

The route Amanda walked to school led her past the Smithtown harbor. Flat pieces of ice floated in the water. A handful of ships were at the docks. They seemed to shiver in the wind.

Amanda pulled her coat tighter around her neck. Just then, she heard a voice call out. A man stood by the docks, waving his arms.

Amanda picked her way down a small hill to where the man was standing. "What's the matter?" she asked.

The man had on a heavy, worn overcoat, boots, and gloves. His wrinkled face was red from the cold. He pointed to the harbor.

Amanda saw water and large, floating platforms of ice. A few sea gulls wheeled through the sky.

"No. Closer, down there," the man said.

A small, brown dog was on one of the patches of ice floating near the dock. The ice was drifting slowly away.

*A man stood by the docks, waving his arms.*

"I'm the night watchman here," the man said. "I just found Queenie out there a moment ago. She must have wandered onto the ice last night. And when the sun came up, the ice broke away. The other workers haven't come in yet. You're the only person I can find."

"What are we going to do?" Amanda asked. There were four feet of water between the dock and the ice that Queenie sat shivering on.

"I've got a ladder. You hold the end up here. I'm going down there." The night watchman poked the foot of the ladder onto the surface of the ice. Amanda took hold of the top.

On the third step down, the watchman's boot slipped on an icy rung. The ladder jolted to one side, and Amanda's feet slipped on the icy boards of the dock.

The watchman slapped a hand over the dock's edge. Amanda caught at the rough cloth of his coat. Slowly, she helped him as he wriggled back onto the dock.

"Are you O.K.?" the watchman asked. His breath came out in short, white clouds.

"I'm all right," said Amanda.

"We'll try again?"

"O.K. Let's go."

The dog and the ice had drifted a few inches farther out. Queenie was watching them now. She had a frightened look in her eyes.

This time, the watchman worked his way down more slowly. As Amanda held the ladder, she started to feel the strain in her arms.

The man took a careful step onto the ice, then another. It seemed to be

*Queenie had a frightened look in her eyes.*

holding. "O.K., Queenie. Steady, girl. I'm coming," he promised.

But Queenie was too scared to understand what was happening. She got up on all four legs. The frightened look in her eyes got worse.

The man was one step away when she ran. She started like a scared rabbit, but her feet slid on the ice. Barking and slipping, she slid toward where the ice ended and the water began.

The watchman dived like a football player trying to stop a touchdown. A hand caught Queenie's leg. Lying flat on the ice, he pulled the rest of Queenie into his arms.

Several dock workers had wandered onto the docks by now. The first ones in had come down beside Amanda. One now held the ladder in two big hands.

The watchman worked his way back

over the ice. Queenie was cradled against his chest, shaking. When the watchman was halfway up the ladder, another worker leaned over and pulled him up. Amanda took Queenie from the watchman's arms. He swung over the last rung and onto the dock.

"That was some tackle Klonsky made," one of the workers shouted. Klonsky was stamping his feet on the dock. Queenie's ears had straightened up. She was starting to enjoy the attention she was getting.

By now, a small crowd of dock workers had gathered. They were making jokes with Klonsky. A few came over and slapped Amanda on the back.

"Where are your manners, Klonsky?" someone asked. "This girl's about to die from the cold." Klonsky took Amanda and Queenie up to the shack he used. It

*Amanda took Queenie from the watchman's arms.*

had a cast-iron stove with a fire going. Klonsky poured coffee into tin cups from the coffeepot on top of the stove.

"Queenie's just a stray that hangs around the docks," he told Amanda. "I feed her scraps of meat and let her get warm now and then. I just like having her around. It helps when it gets lonely."

There was a phone in the shack. Amanda called the *News* office. Luke came down and took pictures. He snapped photos of Klonsky and Queenie, and then Amanda with both of them.

"Mr. Klonsky's a very brave man," Amanda told Luke.

"Yeah, it's a great story," Luke agreed. "The boss will love it. But he told me to ask you something when I was finished."

"What's that?"

"He said to ask if you shouldn't be in school right now," Luke grinned.

"Oh, I almost forgot," said Amanda, smiling back. "I was on my way there."

"I can drive you the rest of the way," Luke offered. "I'll drop you off on my way back to the office."

Amanda accepted, then turned to Queenie. "Look at you," Amanda said. Queenie had curled herself up by the warm stove. "It's a rough life, isn't it, Queenie?"